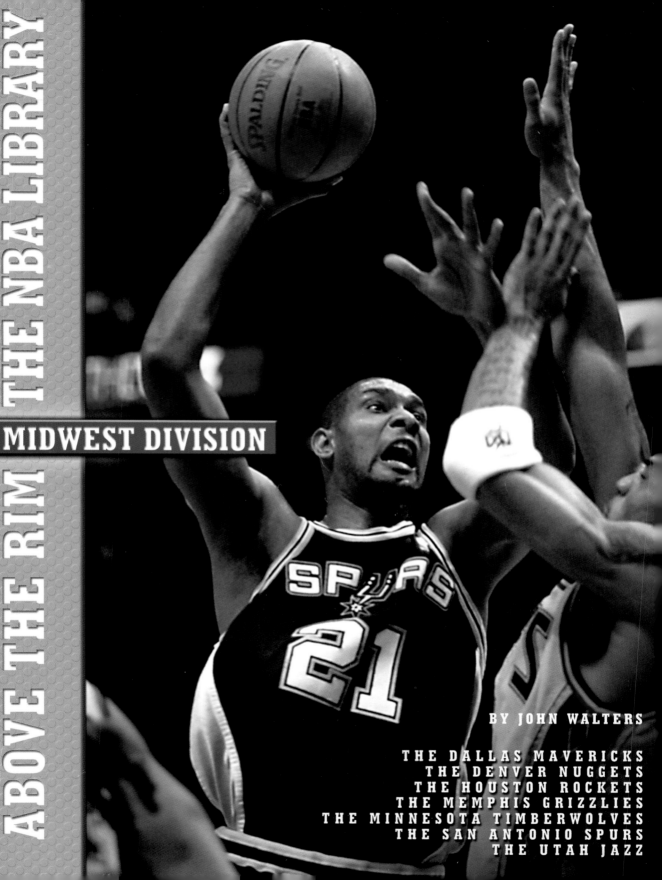

THE NBA LIBRARY

MIDWEST DIVISION

ABOVE THE RIM

BY JOHN WALTERS

THE DALLAS MAVERICKS
THE DENVER NUGGETS
THE HOUSTON ROCKETS
THE MEMPHIS GRIZZLIES
THE MINNESOTA TIMBERWOLVES
THE SAN ANTONIO SPURS
THE UTAH JAZZ

Note to readers:

At press time, the NBA was considering a plan that would reorganize the league into six divisions of five teams, beginning in the 2004-05 season. It will also add a 30th team, the Charlotte Bobcats.

THE MIDWEST DIVISION: The Dallas Mavericks, the Denver Nuggets, the Houston Rockets, the Memphis Grizzlies, the Minnesota Timberwolves, the San Antonio Spurs, and the Utah Jazz

Published in the United States of America by The Child's World®
PO Box 326 • Chanhassen, MN 55317-0326 • 800-599-READ • www.childsworld.com

ACKNOWLEDGEMENTS:
The Child's World®: Mary Berendes, Publishing Director

Editorial Directions, Inc.: E. Russell Primm, Editorial Director and Line Editor; Katie Marsico, Assistant Editor; Matthew Messbarger, Editorial Assistant; Susan Hindman, Copy Editor; Melissa McDaniel, Proofreader; Tim Griffin, Indexer; Kevin Cunningham, Fact Checker; James Buckley Jr., Photo Reseacher and Photo Selector

The Design Lab: Kathleen Petelinsek, Designer and Production Artist

PHOTOS:
Cover: AFP/Corbis
AP/Wide World: 7, 14, 17, 23, 27, 42, 44.
Bettman/Corbis: 9, 10, 12, 20, 24, 29, 30, 33, 38.
Sports Gallery: 18, 35, 40.

LIBRARY OF CONGRESS CATALOGING-IN-PUBLICATION DATA
Walters, John (John Andrew)
The Midwest Division : the Dallas Mavericks, the Denver Nuggets, the Houston Rockets, the Memphis Grizzlies, the Minnesota Timberwolves, the San Antonio Spurs, and the Utah Jazz / by John Walters.
 p. cm. — (Above the rim)
Summary: Describes the seven teams that make up the Midwest Division of the National Basketball Association, their histories, famous players, and statistics.
Includes bibliographical references and index.
 ISBN 1-59296-205-X (lib. bdg. : alk. paper)
1. National Basketball Association—History—Juvenile literature. 2. Basketball—Middle West—History—Juvenile literature. [1. National Basketball Association—History. 2. Basketball.] I. Title. II. Series.
GV885.515.N37W35 2004
796.323'64'0973—dc22
                    2003020033.

Before the 1970–71 season, the National Basketball Association (NBA) added three new teams, expanding from 14 to 17 franchises. Previously, the NBA's 14 teams were placed in either the Eastern Division or Western Division. In 1970–71, however, the NBA made some changes. It doubled from two to four divisions: the Atlantic and Central in the Eastern Conference, and the Midwest and Pacific in the Western Conference.

As the NBA has expanded over the years, 15 different teams have been placed in the Midwest Division. In fact, none of its original four teams currently play there. The Phoenix Suns were moved into the Pacific Division in 1972. The Detroit Pistons were placed in the Central Division in 1978. The Chicago Bulls and the Milwaukee Bucks joined the Pistons there in 1980.

As of the 2003–04 season, seven teams are in the Midwest Division. Three of them are based in Texas and entered the division in 1980. The Houston Rockets and the San Antonio Spurs were moved over from the Central Division. The Dallas Mavericks were an **expansion** franchise that season.

The other four Midwest Division franchises are the Denver Nuggets, the Utah Jazz, the Minnesota Timberwolves, and the Memphis Grizzlies. The Nuggets entered the NBA from the American Basketball Association (ABA) in 1976 and have always been in the Midwest. Denver has the longest tenure of any franchise in the Midwest. The Jazz, originally based in New Orleans, moved to Salt Lake City and the Midwest in 1979.

The "T-Wolves" entered the NBA in 1989 and have always been in the Midwest. The Grizzlies, who were based in Vancouver from 1995 until 2001, have also always been a Midwest Division franchise.

Midwest players and teams have won 10 NBA Most Valuable Player (MVP) awards and five NBA championships. Kareem Abdul-Jabbar was the MVP in 1971, 1972, and 1974 with Milwaukee. Winners Moses Malone (1982) and Hakeem Olajuwon (1994) were both Houston Rockets. David Robinson (1995) and Tim Duncan (2002 and 2003) starred for the San Antonio Spurs. Karl Malone (1997 and 1999) played for the Utah Jazz.

The Bucks were NBA champions in 1971, and the Rockets won it all in 1994 and 1995. The San Antonio Spurs won NBA titles in 1999 and 2003.

TEAM	YEAR FOUNDED	HOME ARENA	YEAR ARENA OPENED	TEAM COLORS
DALLAS MAVERICKS	1980	AMERICAN AIRLINES ARENA	2001	BLUE & GREEN
DENVER NUGGETS	1967	PEPSI CENTER	1999	GOLD, RED, & BLUE
HOUSTON ROCKETS	1967	COMPAQ CENTER	1975	RED, MIDNIGHT BLUE, MERCURY BLUE, & METALLIC SILVER
MEMPHIS GRIZZLIES	1995	FEDEXFORUM	2004	TURQUOISE, RED, BRONZE, & BLACK
MINNESOTA TIMBERWOLVES	1989	TARGET CENTER	1990	BLUE, GREEN, & SILVER
SAN ANTONIO SPURS	1967	SBC CENTER	2002	METALLIC SILVER, BLACK, TEAL, FUCHSIA, & ORANGE
UTAH JAZZ	1974	DELTA CENTER	1991	PURPLE, BLUE, GREEN, COPPER, & BLACK

CHAPTER 1

THE DALLAS MAVERICKS

Three NBA franchises make their home in Texas: the Dallas Mavericks, the Houston Rockets, and the San Antonio Spurs. The "Mavs" are the youngest of the three and the only ones yet to win an NBA championship.

The franchise debuted in the 1980–81 season. Coach Dick Motta, who only two years earlier had guided the Washington Bullets to an NBA title, tried everything to get this new team to win games. Once, during halftime of a game, he entered the locker room with a live tiger to scare the laziness out of his players. Another time, he ordered his center, Wayne Cooper, to **goaltend** a free throw attempt.

Nothing worked. The Mavs finished a league-worst 15–67 in their rookie season. After that, their win totals climbed annually, from 15 to 28 to 38 to 43 to 44. During the 1983–84 season, forward Mark Aguirre finished second in the NBA in scoring (29.5 points per game) and became the first

The Mavericks retired Rolando Blackman's number 22 in 2000.

Maverick All-Star. That season was also the first Dallas made the **playoffs.**

In 1986–87, the Mavs rolled to a 55–27 record and won the Midwest Division. Aguirre and guard Rolando Blackman, both All-Stars who had arrived in Dallas as rookies in the franchise's second season, were the featured players. **Power forward** Sam Perkins was a rising star. Off the bench, the Mavs had two more forwards—7-foot Roy Tarpley and 6-foot-10 Detlef Schrempf—who later in their careers would each win NBA **Sixth Man** of the Year awards.

Dallas beat Seattle 151–129 in the first postsea-

son game that season and then lost three straight.
Motta quit and was replaced by John McLeod, who
led Dallas to a 53-win season in 1987–88. After losing in the playoffs again, the Mavericks went into a
tailspin for a decade. Six different coaches took
their turn on the sideline. In 1992–93, Dallas won
just 11 games, and they began the next season with
a 1–23 record before finishing 13–69. Big "D"
stood for "disaster."

In the early 1990s, Dallas used three consecutive top-10 **draft** picks to select **point guard** Jimmy
Jackson (1992), power forward Jamal Mashburn
(1993), and point guard Jason Kidd (1994). Hailed
as the "Three Js," this trio was supposed to return
the Mavericks to glory. Alas, the Three Js began to
stand for Jealousy, Juvenile, and Jinxed. Jackson,
Mashburn, and Kidd feuded off the court and had
trouble sharing the ball on it. The Mavericks even-
tually traded all three of them. Dallas also traded
Tony Dumas and Loren Meyer. They got Michael
Finley, Sam Cassell, and A. C. Green.

In 1998, forward Dirk Nowitzki, just 20 years
old and 7 feet tall, arrived from Germany. Nowitzki
plays a nearly flawless game and has a deadly out-

Dirk Nowitzki combines a big man's size with a shooter's touch.

Steve Nash came to Dallas from north of the border.

side shot that, because of his height, is virtually unblockable. By the 2002–03 season, Nowitzki had established himself as a star, ranking in the league's top 10 in both scoring and rebounding.

Finley, Steve Nash (a Canadian with a rock-star persona), and Nowitzki have become the trio that Dallas had hoped the Three Js would be. Dallas, with a potent, pass-happy offense, has become one of the league's most entertaining teams. They have also, under the tutelage of coach Don Nelson, become one of the best. The Mavs won 53 games in 2000–01 and a franchise-record 57 in 2001–02. In the 2002–03 season, Dallas burst out of the gates 14–0 before finishing the regular season tied for the best record in the NBA, 60–22, a franchise first.

On February 23, 2002, against the Sacramento Kings, Dirk Nowitzki set an NBA record for the most defensive rebounds in a game (21) without an offensive rebound.

THE DENVER NUGGETS

In 1976, the ABA took its red, white, and blue basketball and went home. After nine seasons, the ABA—famous for this tri-colored ball, which it used instead of the traditional orange one—**disbanded.** Four of its franchises—the Denver Nuggets, the Indiana Pacers, the New York Nets, and the San Antonio Spurs—joined the NBA. The Nuggets were among the best of the ABA refugees.

Denver went 50–32 and won the Midwest Division in 1976–77. That team boasted three stars: center Dan Issel, forward Bobby Jones, and guard David "Skywalker" Thompson, who earned his nickname from his gravity-defying dunks. Thompson was also a prolific scorer. Four times, he finished among the top six in the league in scoring. The Nuggets, however, became linked to scoring and letdowns. Coach Doug Moe arrived in 1981, and in his first full season, 1981–82, the Nuggets established a new NBA mark for scoring, averaging 126.5 points per game. Unfortunately, they set another record for

High-flying David Thompson was nicknamed "Skywalker."

points allowed, 126.0 per game. They are still the only team to score at least 100 points in all 82 games of a season. They also surrendered at least 100 points in every game, finishing 46–36.

The 1982–83 Nuggets were about the same. Forwards Alex English (28.4 points per game) and Kiki Vandeweghe (26.7) finished 1–2 in the NBA in scoring, but the Nuggets, 45–37, were eliminated in the second round of playoffs by San Antonio. During the 1983–84 season, they scored 184 points in three overtimes against the Pistons—and lost, 186–184.

Moe departed in 1990. His replacement, Paul Westhead, promised just as much offense. But again, the Nuggets played poor defense. They started out 0–7, surrendering no fewer than 135 points in any of the losses. In one of them, the Phoenix Suns torched Denver for 107 first-half points, an NBA record. Denver again allowed 100 points in all 82 games (no other franchise has ever done that) and set a record for points allowed per game, 130.8. That 1990–91 team finished 20–62, last in the league.

Since then, Denver has finished above .500 once. One highlight was the play of Dikembe Mutombo, a 7-foot-2 center from the Democratic

Of the four ABA expansion franchises that entered the NBA in 1976, the Nuggets are the only ones to never advance to the NBA Finals. Denver's first trip to the Western Conference finals was during the 1977–78 season. During their second trip, in 1985, the Los Angeles Lakers— averaging more than 132 points per contest—beat them 4–1.

Republic of the Congo. He led the league in blocked shots for three consecutive seasons, was twice named to the All-Star team, and was named the league's Defensive Player of the Year for the 1994–95 season. In 1994, the number-eight seeded Nuggets defeated the number-one seeded Seattle SuperSonics in the playoffs. No eighth-seeded team has beaten a number-one seed, before or since.

Except for a notably disastrous 11–71 season in 1997–98, the Nuggets have largely been forgotten by the rest of the league.

Rookie Carmelo Anthony (right) gives Denver hope for the future.

THE HOUSTON ROCKETS

For 27 seasons, the Houston Rockets had the reputation of being a solid franchise, but one that couldn't quite make it into championship orbit. Then, in the mid-1990s, while Chicago's Michael Jordan was off playing baseball, the Rockets won a pair of NBA titles.

The franchise began in 1967 as the San Diego Rockets. Their first draft pick that season was Pat Riley, who would go on to greater success as a coach than as a player. San Diego finished the season with the NBA's worst record, 15–67.

Rewarded with the top overall pick in the 1968 draft, San Diego chose Elvin Hayes. As a rookie, "the Big E" led the NBA in scoring (28.4 points per game) and was fourth in rebounding. Hayes, a 6-foot-10 power forward, finished in the top three in the league in both scoring and rebounding the next two seasons. Before his fourth season, 1971–72, the Rockets moved to Houston, where the Big E had attended college. The Rockets did not have a permanent home arena, however, so they often played home games in smaller south-western cities. Hayes averaged a team-best 25.2 points per game that year.

Two of his teammates would become the most popular players in franchise history. Rudy Tomjanovich, a sweet-shooting 6-foot-8 forward, would later coach Houston to their championships. Calvin Murphy, a 5-foot-9 dynamo, would retire as the franchise's all-time leading scorer. Both spent their entire careers in Rockets' uniforms.

In 1972, the NBA moved the franchise from the Western Conference to the Central Division in the Eastern Conference. There they remained for eight seasons, until 1980–81, when the league re-relo-cated them to the Midwest Division.

The move agreed with the Rockets, who despite a 40–42 record, advanced all the way to the NBA Finals. Though the Rockets boasted 6-foot-10 center Moses Malone (who would end his career with three MVP trophies), the Celtics ended the Rockets' unlikely championship run in six games.

In both 1983 and 1984, the Rockets had the number-one overall picks in the NBA draft. They

Moses Malone was so talented he went from high school to the NBA.

chose 7-foot-4 Ralph Sampson and 6-foot-10 Olajuwon, respectively. The "Twin Towers," as this pair became known, returned the Rockets to the NBA Finals in 1986. Again, Houston stunned a defending champion Lakers team. To win Game 5, Sampson made a famous off-balance **buzzer-beater.** Houston, however, once again fell to the Celtics in the finals.

Over the next decade, Olajuwon, a Nigerian native who had played soccer—not basketball—as a youth, became the league's dominant center. He was graceful and, thanks to his soccer background, blessed with extraordinary footwork in the **low post.**

During the 1992–93 season, Charles Barkley

Rudy Tomjanovich was the victim of the most violent on-court act in NBA history. In December 1977, a fight broke out between Kermit Washington of the Los Angeles Lakers and Kevin Kunnert of the Houston Rockets. Tomjanovich ran over to the fracas, whereupon Washington, a karate expert, wheeled around and punched him in the face. Tomjanovich suffered massive facial injuries and missed the rest of the season.

Hakeem was "The Dream" for Rockets' fans.

was the defending MVP. In 1993–94, Olajuwon, known as "the Dream," earned the honor. In the NBA Finals, the Rockets faced the New York Knicks, who had the league's next-best center of the era, Patrick Ewing. Olajuwon averaged 26.9 points, 9.1 rebounds, and 3.9 blocked shots against Ewing. The Rockets won the series, 4–3, at last bringing a championship to Houston.

In 1995, Olajuwon was joined by his former University of Houston teammate, Clyde "the Glide" Drexler. Together, they helped Houston through a difficult postseason. To win their second straight championship, the Rockets had to defeat four 55-win teams, all of which had **homecourt advantage:** the Utah Jazz, the Phoenix Suns, the San Antonio Spurs, and the Orlando Magic.

With a supporting cast that included Robert Horry, Sam Cassell, and Kenny Smith, the Rockets prevailed. Houston faced elimination games five times, winning all five. Only the finals, in which Olajuwon outclassed budding star Shaquille O'Neal of the Magic, were a breather. Houston swept Orlando, 4–0.

Olajuwon, who left Houston for the Toronto

On and off the court, Yao Ming is one of the league's biggest stars.

Raptors after the 2000–01 season, has compiled career numbers that place him among the best players in league history. He is in the all-time top 10 in scoring and 11th in rebounding. He is the only center in the top 10 in steals and is the NBA's all-time blocked shots leader.

In 2002, the Rockets once again drafted a foreign-born center. Yao Ming, from China, is 7-foot-5. So far, Yao appears to have the same type of skills and personality as Olajuwon. Time will tell if Houston has another Dream on its hands—and for the rest of the NBA, a recurring nightmare.

THE MEMPHIS GRIZZLIES

In 1995, the Toronto Raptors and the Vancouver Grizzlies became the first NBA franchises to be based outside of the United States since the Toronto Huskies folded in 1947. The Grizzlies finished in last place in the Midwest Division in their debut season. Their 15–67 record was the league's worst.

The season actually began well. Vancouver won its inaugural game, 92–80, at Portland. They followed that victory with a 100–98 home debut defeat of the Minnesota Timberwolves.

Then reality hit. Vancouver lost 19 straight games, including a 49-point loss at San Antonio. Coach Brian Winters depended on a few savvy veterans, such as guards Greg Anthony (the team's leading scorer at 14.0 points per game) and Byron Scott, as well as 7-foot rookie center Bryant "Big Country" Reeves. The Grizzlies simply had a shortage of talent, and they later lost 23 consecutive games that first season.

Selecting third in the 1996 NBA draft, Vancouver chose 6-foot-9 forward Shareef Abdur-Rahim. The former University of California star had left Berkeley after becoming the first freshman in Pac-10 history to be named the conference's player of the year. He immediately became Vancouver's go-to player. He averaged 18.7 points per game in 1996–97, tops on the club. Instead of improving, though, Vancouver sank to 14–68 and again had the poorest record in the NBA.

In those early seasons, Vancouver's year-end win-loss records resembled dates on a history quiz: 15–67, 14–68, 19–63 and, in the strike-shortened 1999 season, 8–42. Abdur-Rahim did his best on poor teams. In 1998, his 22.3 points per game ranked sixth in the league.

Vancouver, in the province of British Columbia, is about three hours north of Seattle by car. Fans initially supported the team. Still, many players considered it to be the NBA's farthest **outpost.**

In 1998, the Grizzlies used the second pick in the draft to take Mike Bibby, a gifted point guard. In 1999, they chose shooting guard Steve Francis from the University of Maryland. Francis immedi-

Even Michael Jordan (left) knows that Shane Battier is one to watch.

ately declared that he would never play for Vancouver, which left the franchise in a tight spot. They traded Francis (who would go on to share the NBA Rookie of the Year title) to Houston and received Bibby's former University of Arizona teammate Michael Dickerson, three other players, and a future draft pick in return.

That season, 1999–2000, Vancouver finished last in the Midwest (22–60) for the fourth time in its five years of existence. After the 2000–01 season, Bibby headed south to play for the Sacramento

Five current Grizzlies are former All-Rookie first team members: Shane Battier, Pau Gasol, Brevin Knight, Mike Miller, and Jason Williams.

Spain's Pau Gasol has made a big impact since coming to Memphis.

Kings. With attendance heading in the same direction, Vancouver decided to move the entire franchise south—to Memphis. Abdur-Rahim, the nearest thing to a star that the franchise had, was traded to the Atlanta Hawks.

The Memphis Grizzlies were almost an entirely new team, in an entirely new location. New general manager Jerry West shrewdly acquired a high draft pick for Abdur-Rahim so that on draft day of 2001, Memphis had two of the first six picks. They drafted 7-foot forward Pau Gasol from Spain and 6-foot-10 forward Shane Battier, the national college player of the year, from Duke University.

Both Gasol and Battier were named to the All-Rookie first team. Gasol averaged 17.6 points and 8.9 rebounds per game and was the 2002 Rookie of the Year.

Slowly but surely, the Grizzlies have improved. In 2002–03, West traded for 2001 Rookie of the Year Mike Miller. Aided by the talents of point guard Jason Williams and center Strohmile Swift, the 2003 Grizzlies won a franchise-record 28 games. Migrating south and adding West were both moves in the right direction.

The 2002–03 Grizzlies began the season with 13 straight losses. In March, they went on the longest winning streak in franchise history—six games.

THE MINNESOTA TIMBERWOLVES

T he history of the Minnesota Timber-wolves can easily be divided into two eras: pre-Kevin Garnett and post- Kevin Garnett. Before the gifted Garnett arrived in 1995 straight out of high school, the T-Wolves were a typical expansion ball club. Their limited talent could barely win 25 games in a season. Since Garnett donned a Minnesota jersey, however, the T-Wolves have become an attraction wherever they play, and they regularly visit the postseason.

The Minnesota franchise came into being in 1989. The state's 842 city councils voted for the name Timberwolves over the other choice, Polars. The T-Wolves began play in the Metrodome, home to the Minnesota Twins and Vikings. Minnesota had not had an NBA franchise since the Minneapolis Lakers, who won five NBA titles, moved to Los Angeles following the 1958–59 season.

The T-Wolves made their NBA debut at home before 35,427 fans. They lost to the Chicago Bulls

96–84, as Michael
Jordan drained 45
points. It would take
15 more losses and
eight seasons before
Minnesota would at
last defeat Chicago.

The fans were
Minnesota's MVP dur-
ing the inaugural
22–60 campaign. On
April 17, 1990, for the
final home game,

Tom Gugliotta was one of the franchise's first true stars.

49,551 fans swept through the turnstiles. That
crowd, the third-largest for a single game in NBA history, allowed Minnesota to establish a new single-sea-
son attendance record average of 26,160 fans per
game. The following season, Minnesota moved into
their new and current home, the Target Center.

Those early T-Wolves teams were neither good
nor easy to cheer for. Christian Laettner, Minnesota's top pick in the 1992 draft and the only
collegiate member of America's first Olympic
"Dream Team," always wore a scowl. He was once

suspended for a game for screaming at an assistant coach during a practice.

The following season, Minnesota used its first pick to select Isaiah Rider. He arrived late for his own introductory press conference. Things went downhill from there.

In 1995, Kevin Garnett, a senior at Farragut Academy in Chicago, made himself eligible for the NBA draft. Many teams were skeptical; 20 years had passed since a high school player had jumped directly to the NBA. Kevin McHale, the former Boston Celtics' Hall of Fame forward who was then (and still is) the T-Wolves' general manager, took a chance on Garnett. He selected the 18-year-old with the fifth overall pick in the draft.

McHale's gamble has paid off. Garnett, the proto-type of the modern player, is nearly 7 feet tall (he's 6-11), but can dribble like a point guard, shoot like an off-guard, and rebound and defend like a power forward. In his first eight seasons, he has been named to the All-Star team six times. In 2003, he was named MVP of the All-Star contest in Atlanta.

In 1996, Minnesota drafted guard Ray Allen and then traded Allen and a draft pick for point

The Timberwolves' success begins and ends with Kevin Garnett.

guard Stephon Marbury. Coached by Flip Saunders,
Minnesota cleared three hurdles during the
1996–97 season: The T-Wolves beat Chicago for the
first time, they had their first All-Star representa-
tives (forwards Tom Gugliotta and Kevin Garnett),
and they advanced to the playoffs with a 40–42
record. Minnesota, however, was swept by the
Houston Rockets in the first round, 3–0.

In 1999, the realities of NBA payrolls and ego
caused the franchise to take a step backward.

Before that season,
Garnett had been
signed to the largest
contract in NBA his-
tory, worth approxi-
mately $120 million.
Jealousy ensued.

Marbury, light-
ning-quick and a great
assists player, was
unhappy about playing
second fiddle to
Garnett. He was trad-
ed to the New Jersey

Wally Szczerbiak has helped the
Timberwolves make major strides.

Nets midway through the season. Gugliotta, a free agent, signed with the Phoenix Suns before the season began, for far more cash than McHale was willing—or able—to pay him. (Marbury flourished in New Jersey, finishing among the top 10 in the league in both scoring and assists.) Minnesota obtained steady Terrell Brandon to replace Marbury. At power forward, Joe Smith, who had been the first player taken in the 1995 draft (four spots ahead of Garnett), replaced Gugliotta. Minnesota stumbled, however, finishing 25–25.

The following season the T-Wolves drafted a legitimate second scoring option. Wally Szczerbiak, a 6-foot-7 forward, was named to the All-Rookie first team. He is a career 15-points-per-game scorer and, after Garnett, has become the T-Wolves' most vital player.

The Timberwolves have qualified for the postseason in the talent-rich Western Conference every season since 1997. With Garnett and Szczerbiak on board, Minnesota has won at least 50 games in three of the past four seasons. The next step as the franchise matures is for the T-Wolves to win a playoff series.

CHAPTER 6

THE SAN ANTONIO SPURS

Since joining the NBA prior to the 1976–77 season, the San Antonio Spurs have consistently been a winner. Only three times in their NBA history have the Spurs failed to win at least 30 games.

The Spurs were born in 1967, in a different Texas town in a different league. A charter member of the ABA, the Spurs began as the Dallas Chaparrals. The franchise moved to San Antonio in 1973. It was renamed the Spurs.

In 1976, San Antonio became one of four teams from the ABA to join the NBA and was placed in the Central Division. The team's big star was silky smooth 6-foot-8 shooter George Gervin. "The Iceman," as he was known, was an incredible scoring machine.

With his patented **finger-roll** and deadly jumper, the Iceman led the league in scoring in four different seasons (only Wilt Chamberlain and Michael Jordan have claimed more scoring titles). He once

scored 63 points on
the final day of one
season to win a scor-
ing title by less than
.10 points per game.
His most prolific scor-
ing season was
1979–80, when he
averaged 33.1 points
per game.

Gervin helped the
Spurs to the playoffs
in 1979, but the result
was heartbreaking.
The Spurs led the
Eastern Conference

"The Iceman," George Gervin,
won four NBA scoring titles.

finals three games to one but then lost three
straight. The final loss, a 107–105 pulse-racer, ended
when Washington's Elvin Hayes blocked Spurs guard
James Silas' shot at the buzzer.

That was as close as Spurs' fans came to seeing
a championship for a long time. San Antonio moved
to the Midwest Division in the Western Conference
in 1980. The Spurs won three consecutive division

titles. Gervin's scoring, however, paled against the many weapons of the Los Angeles Lakers, who routed San Antonio in the Western Conference finals in both 1982 and 1983.

In 1987, San Antonio, picking first in the NBA draft for the very first time, selected 7-foot center David Robinson from the United States Naval Academy. But the Spurs had to wait for "the Admiral" to fulfill a two-year military commitment before he could join the league.

In 1989, Robinson did start play, along with forward Sean Elliott. Two of the league's best community leaders off the court, as well as All-Stars on it, Robinson and Elliott reversed the franchise's course. San Antonio went from 21 wins the previous season to 56 the next. The 35-victory leap was an NBA record. The Admiral, averaging 24.3 points, 12.0 rebounds, and 3.89 blocked shots per game, was a shoo-in for Rookie of the Year.

In 1994–95, the Admiral steered the franchise to uncharted waters. For the first time, San Antonio finished with the league's best record, 62–20. Robinson became the Spurs' first league MVP, averaging 27.6 points per contest.

David Robinson capped a great career with an NBA title in 2003.

Before the 1998–99 season, the Spurs chose
7-footer Tim Duncan, a native of the U.S. Virgin
Islands. Blessed with a graceful bank shot and a
calm manner, Duncan teamed with Robinson and
Elliott to give San Antonio a **formidable frontcourt.** It
was perhaps the NBA's best since the Boston
Celtics' trio of Hall of Famers (Larry Bird, Kevin
McHale, and Robert Parish) a decade earlier.

Duncan followed in the Admiral's footsteps, winning the Rookie of the Year award in 1998 and MVP
in 2002 and 2003. In 1998–99, Duncan was among
the league leaders in scoring and rebounding as San
Antonio won its first NBA championship.

The Spurs were magnificent that postseason.
San Antonio, which shared the league's top regular-
season record (37–13) with the Utah Jazz, swept
two series and finished 15–2 overall in the playoffs.
In the NBA Finals, they defeated the New York
Knicks, 4–1.

In 2002–03, Robinson's last season, San
Antonio won its second title. On the way, the Spurs
defeated the three-time defending champion
Lakers. In the finals, they downed the New Jersey
Nets, four games to two.

THE UTAH JAZZ

I f you were to create an all-time All-NBA team strictly by the five positions (point guard, shooting guard, small forward, power forward, and center), you could make a strong argument that two of the five players would be Karl Malone and John Stockton of the Utah Jazz.

Stockton, a point guard, was drafted by the Jazz in 1984. Malone, a power forward, was selected by the Jazz in 1985. Through the 2002–03 season, the pair were teammates. Then Stockton retired, and Malone signed with the Lakers as a free agent. But no two players have remained together on the same team for a longer period (18 seasons) in league history.

Individually, Stockton and Malone have rewritten the NBA record book. The 6-foot-1, clean-cut Stockton is the league's all-time leader in assists (15,806) and steals (3,625). Stockton led the NBA in assists for nine straight seasons, a league record, from 1988 to 1996. Most experts consider either

Point guard John Stockton passed his way into the NBA record book.

Stockton or Earvin "Magic" Johnson to be the greatest point guard ever.

Malone, at 6-foot-9, is number one all-time in free throws made (9,619) and attempted (12,963) as well as defensive rebounds (11,100). "The Mailman," as he is known, is number two in career scoring (36,374 points), trailing only Kareem Abdul-Jabbar. Malone, who won the league MVP award in 1997 and 1999, is simply the best power forward ever to lace up a pair of sneakers.

Stockton and Malone led the Jazz to five Midwest Division titles (they tied for a sixth in 1989–90 with San Antonio) and two trips to the NBA Finals. Those journeys, in 1997 and 1998, were spoiled by the incomparable Michael Jordan and the Chicago Bulls. But no team ever put more of a scare into the Bulls than the Jazz.

The Jazz came into the league as an expansion franchise, the New Orleans Jazz, in 1974. The marquee player was "Pistol" Pete Maravich, a superior passer and shooter. Pistol Pete led the league in scoring in 1976–77 by averaging 31.1 points per game. On one evening that season, Maravich scored 68 points against the New York Knicks.

In 1979, the Jazz moved to Salt Lake City and the Midwest Division. The key players there included forward Darrell Griffith, alias "Dr. Dunkenstein." He was the 1981 Rookie of the Year. Though only 6-foot-5, forward Adrian Dantley powered to the hoop enough times to twice lead the league in scoring, in 1980–81 and 1983–84.

The 1983–84 season was one of many firsts for the Jazz. Led by colorful coach Frank Layden, Utah won the Midwest Division (45–37) for the first

On November 27, 1996, the Jazz posted the greatest comeback in NBA history. Utah trailed the Denver Nuggets by 36 points but rallied to win, 107–103.

The Jazz hold the team record for most consecutive free throws made in a game: 39. Utah set the record playing the Portland Trail Blazers on December 7, 1982.

Karl Malone was called "The Mailman"
because he always delivered.

time. Layden wore outlandish clothes, weighed somewhere above 300 pounds, and always had fun. Once, as the Jazz were being creamed by the Los Angeles Lakers, Layden left the arena. As his team was playing out the final minutes, Layden could be seen eating a sandwich at the hotel coffee shop.

During that 1983–84 season, the Jazz also became the first and only team to have four different players lead the league in a major statistical category. Besides Dantley, Griffith had the highest percentage in the NBA in three-point field-goals (.361). Guard Rickey Green led the league in steals (2.65 per game). Big 7-foot-4 center Mark Eaton led the league in blocks (4.28 per game).

Jerry Sloan, who once played for Chicago, succeeded Layden as coach in 1988, and he has been as permanent a resident with the Jazz as Stockton and Malone.

In the early 1990s, Utah was a terrific team that was never able to clear the hurdle of a Western Conference title. Finally, in 1997, the Jazz did just that. Stockton's buzzer-beating three-pointer in Game 6 of the conference finals against the Houston Rockets sent the Jazz into the NBA Finals.

Mark Eaton was a limited offensive player who did not even start while at UCLA. Still, Eaton led the NBA in blocks in four different seasons and was named Defensive Player of the Year twice.

Of his numerous honors, Karl Malone was twice an All-Star Game MVP (once co-MVP with John Stockton) and has been named to the first-team All-NBA more times (11) than anyone else in league history.

In Utah, the torch has been passed to young stars such as Matt Harpring.

In both 1997 and 1998, the Jazz met the Bulls for the NBA championship. Both years, Utah pushed Chicago to six games. Also in both years, a heroic effort by Michael Jordan made the difference.

While never winning a ring, Stockton, Malone, and Sloan set an unofficial NBA record for sustained excellence. From 1988–89, their first season together, through 2002–03, the Jazz did not suffer a losing season.

TEAM RECORDS

TEAM	ALL-TIME RECORD	NBA TITLES (MOST RECENT)	NUMBER OF TIMES IN PLAYOFFS	TOP COACH (WINS)
DALLAS	814–1,040	0	9	DICK MOTTA (329)
DENVER	1,394–1,532	0	*21	DOUG MOE (432)
HOUSTON	1,447–1,473	2 (1994–95)	21	RUDY TOMJANOVICH (503)
MEMPHIS	152–472	0	0	SIDNEY LOWE (46)
MINNESOTA	460–656	0	7	FLIP SAUNDERS (328)
SAN ANTONIO	1,634–1,292	1 (1998–99)	*31	GREGG POPOVICH (339)
UTAH	1,279–1,067	0	20	JERRY SLOAN (781)

*includes ABA

NBA MIDWEST CAREER LEADERS (THROUGH 2002–03)

TEAM	CATEGORY	NAME (YEARS WITH TEAM)	TOTAL
DALLAS	POINTS	ROLANDO BLACKMAN (1981–92)	16,643
	REBOUNDS	JAMES DONALDSON (1985–92)	4,589
DENVER	POINTS	ALEX ENGLISH (1980–90)	21,645
	REBOUNDS	DAN ISSEL (1975–85)	6,630
HOUSTON	POINTS	HAKEEM OLAJUWON (1984–2001)	26,511
	REBOUNDS	HAKEEM OLAJUWON (1984–2001)	13,382
MEMPHIS	POINTS	SHAREEF ABDUR-RAHIM (1996–2001)	7,801
	REBOUNDS	SHAREEF ABDUR-RAHIM (1996–2001)	3,070
MINNESOTA	POINTS	KEVIN GARNETT (1995–PRESENT)	11,877
	REBOUNDS	KEVIN GARNETT (1995–PRESENT)	6,354
SAN ANTONIO	POINTS	DAVID ROBINSON (1989–2003)	20,790
	REBOUNDS	DAVID ROBINSON (1989–2003)	10,497
UTAH	POINTS	KARL MALONE (1985–2003)	36,374
	REBOUNDS	KARL MALONE (1985–2003)	14,601

MEMBERS OF THE NAISMITH MEMORIAL NATIONAL BASKETBALL HALL OF FAME

DENVER

PLAYER	POSITION	DATE INDUCTED
Alex English	Forward	1997
Dan Issel	Center	1993
John McLendon	Coach	1979
David Thompson	Guard	1996

SAN ANTONIO

PLAYER	POSITION	DATE INDUCTED
George Gervin	Forward	1996
Cliff Hagan	Forward	1978
Moses Malone	Center	2001

HOUSTON

PLAYER	POSITION	DATE INDUCTED
Rick Barry	Guard	1987
Alex Hannum	Coach	1998
Moses Malone	Forward/Center	2001
Calvin Murphy	Guard	1993

UTAH

PLAYER	POSITION	DATE INDUCTED
Pete Maravich	Guard	1987

Note: Dallas, Memphis, and Minnesota do not have any members of the Hall of Fame (yet!).

Pete Maravich

GLOSSARY

buzzer-beater—a shot that wins a game just as the game-ending buzzer sounds

disbanded—broken up, shut down

draft—an annual selection of college players by a pro sports league

expansion—in sports, this means a team created from scratch and added to a league

finger-roll—a type of shot made close to the basket in which the player reaches high over his head and rolls the ball off his fingertips into the basket

formidable—powerful, not easily defeated

frontcourt—term for the forwards and center on a basketball team

goaltend—to block a shot as it is coming down toward the basket; this is an illegal play and the referees will award the basket and the points to the shooting team

homecourt advantage—what a team has when it will play more games in a playoff series at its home arena; most teams have greater success playing in front of their home fans

low post—the area beneath and around the basket, where taller players do most of their work

NBA Finals—a seven-game series between the winners of the NBA's Eastern and Western Conference championships

outpost—an outlying branch of an organization, in this case the NBA

playoffs—a four-level postseason elimination tournament involving eight teams from each conference; levels include two rounds of divisional playoffs (best of five games and best of seven), a conference championship round (best of seven), and the NBA Finals (best of seven)

point guard—a player with ball-handling and passing skills who usually brings the ball upcourt for his team

power forward—a tall, strong player who is depended on for scoring and rebounding

sixth man—term for a team's top substitute, usually the first player into the game after the starting five

TIME LINE

1967 Denver, Houston, and San Antonio begin play in the American Basketball Association (ABA)

1971 Milwaukee wins the NBA title

1974 The Utah Jazz are founded

1976 Four ABA teams join the NBA

1980 The Dallas Mavericks join the NBA as an expansion team

1989 The Minnesota Timberwolves join the NBA

1994–95 The Houston Rockets win consecutive NBA championships

1995 The Memphis Grizzlies are founded (as the Vancouver Grizzlies)

1999 San Antonio captures the NBA title

2003 San Antonio wins its second NBA championship

FOR MORE INFORMATION ABOUT THE MIDWEST DIVISION AND THE NBA

BOOKS

Lace, William W. *The Houston Rockets Basketball Team.* Springfield, N.J.: Enslow Publishers, 1997.

Rogers, Glenn. *The San Antonio Spurs Basketball Team.* Springfield, N.J.: Enslow Publishers, 1997.

Schnakenberg, Robert E. *Teammates: Karl Malone and John Stockton.* Brookfield, Conn.: Millbrook Press, 1998.

ON THE WEB

Visit our home page for lots of links about Midwest Division teams:

http://www.childsworld.com/links.html

NOTE TO PARENTS, TEACHERS, AND LIBRARIANS: We routinely check our Web links to make sure they're safe, active sites—so encourage your readers to check them out!

INDEX

ABOUT THE AUTHOR

John Walters is a former staff writer at *Sports Illustrated* who worked at the magazine from 1989 to 2001. He is the author of two other books, *Basketball for Dummies*, which he cowrote with former Notre Dame basketball coach Digger Phelps, and *The Same River Twice: A Season with Geno Auriemma and the Connecticut Huskies*, which chronicles the women's basketball team's 2000–01 season.